Don't Let the Pigeon Stay Up Late!

words and pictures by mo willems

HYPERION BOOKS FOR CHILDREN / New York
An Imprint of Disney Book Group

For Trixie at bedtime

All rights reserved for humans, not pigeons. Published by Hyperion Books for Children, an imprint of Disney Book Group. No part of this book may be reproduced or transmitted in any form or by any means, electronic or mechanical, including photocopying, recording, or by any information storage and retrieval system, without written permission from the publisher. For information address Hyperion Books for Children, 125 West End Avenue, New York, New York 10023.

First Edition, April 2006

Reinforced binding

20 19 18

FAC-029191-17194

Printed in Malaysia

Library of Congress Cataloging-in-Publication Data on file.

ISBN 13 : 978-0-7868-3746-5

ISBN 10 : 0-7868-3746-2

Visit www.hyperionbooksforchildren.com and www.pigeonpresents.com

Thanks.

→Yawn←

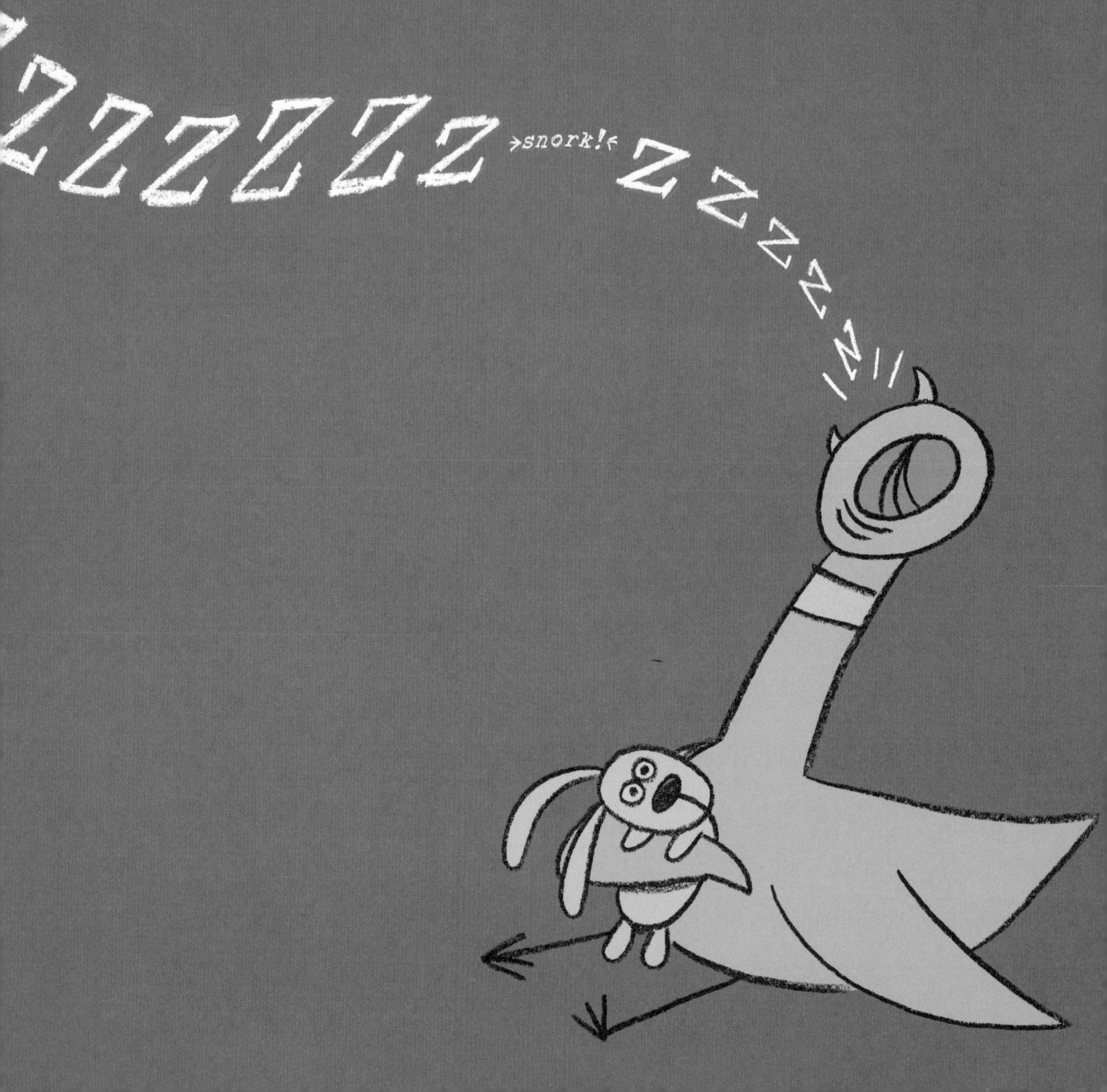
ZZZZZZz
snork!
Z Z Z Z Z